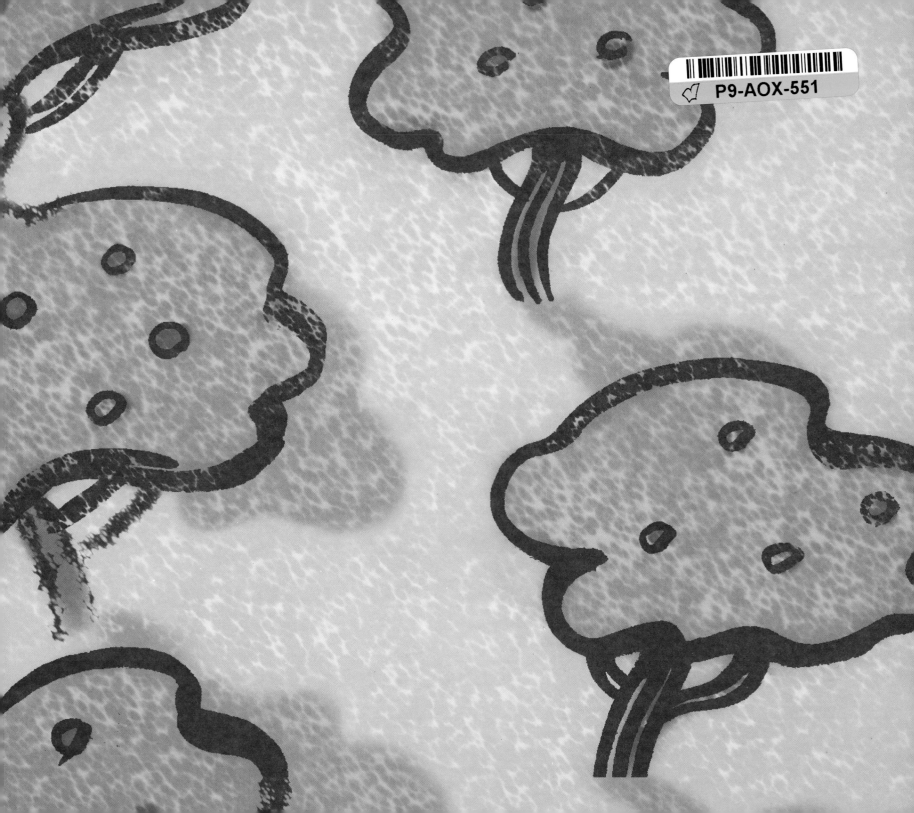

We'll All Go Exploring

Published in Canada by Fitzhenry & Whiteside,
195 Allstate Parkway, Markham, Ontario L3R 4T8

Published in the United States by Fitzhenry & Whiteside,
121 Harvard Avenue, Suite 2, Allston, Massachusetts 02134

www.fitzhenry.ca   godwit@fitzhenry.ca.

10 9 8 7 6 5 4 3 2 1

National Library of Canada Cataloguing in Publication
Spicer, Maggee
We'll all go exploring / by Maggee Spicer and Richard Thompson; illustrated by Kim LaFave.
ISBN 1-55041-732-0 (bound).—ISBN 1-55041-701-0 (pbk.)
1. Forests and forestry—Juvenile poetry. 2. Forest ecology—Juvenile
poetry. 3. Children's poetry, Canadian (English) I. Thompson, Richard, 1951- II. LaFave, Kim III. Title.
PS8587.P498W433 2003   jC811'.54   C2002-905303-X
PZ7

U.S. Publisher Cataloging-in-Publication Data
(Library of Congress Standards)
Spicer, Maggee.
We'll all go exploring : a first flight level one reader / by Maggee Spicer ; Richard Thompson ; [illustrated by] Kim
LaFave. — 1st ed.
[32] p. : col. ill. ; cm.
Summary: Three friends explore the world's forests, visiting different landscapes—pine and deciduous forests,
mangrove swamps, tropical jungles and many more. When they are through, the three friends
leave the forests as they found them, so you too can visit one day.
ISBN1-550471-732-0   ISBN1-550471-701-0 (pbk.)
1. Friends — Fiction. 2. Exploring — Fiction. 3. Wilderness areas — Fiction. I. Thompson, Richard. 2. LaFave, Kim. 3. Title.
[E] 21 2003 AC CIP

Fitzhenry & Whiteside acknowledges with thanks the Canada Council for the Arts,
the Government of Canada through the Book Publishing Industry Development Program (BPIDP),
and the Ontario Arts Council for their support for our publishing program.

Design by Wycliffe Smith Design Inc.
Printed in Hong Kong

To Chie
—Richard and Maggee

To Zach, Ben and Jeff
—Kim

We'll All Go Exploring

By Maggee Spicer and Richard Thompson

ILLUSTRATED BY KIM LaFave

Fitzhenry & Whiteside

We'll all go exploring
In the world of trees,

My friend, Maggee,
And Jesse and me.

With their trunks and limbs,
With their roots and leaves...

Exploring together
Through the land of trees.

We'll all go exploring
Through the autumn trees,

And what will we see
In the trees, we three?

A quick-dart squirrel
And a chickadee!

That's what we'll see
In the autumn trees.

We'll all go exploring
In the dark spruce trees,

And what will we see
In the trees, we three?

A beaver, a moose,
And a Canada goose!

That's what we'll see
In the dark spruce trees.

We'll all go exploring
In the redwood trees,

And what will we see
In the trees, we three?

A marbled murrelet
And a spotted owl!

That's what we'll see
In the redwood trees.

We'll all go exploring
Through the old gum trees,

And what will we see
In the trees, we three?

A kookabura
And a koala bear!

That's what we'll see
In the old gum trees.

We'll all go exploring
Through the piñon trees,

And what will we see
In the trees, we three?

A swift road runner
And a rattlesnake!

That's what we'll see
In the piñon trees.

We'll all go exploring
Through the jungle trees,

And what will we see
In the trees, we three?

A spider monkey
And a lone jaguar!

That's what we'll see
In the jungle trees.

We'll all go exploring
Through the mangrove trees,

And what will we see
In the trees, we three?

A pink flamingo
And a crocodile!

That's what we'll see
In the mangrove trees.

We'll all go exploring
Through the apple trees,

And what will we see
In the trees, we three?

A raccoon bandit
And a hungry crow!

That's what we'll see
In the apple trees.

We'll all go exploring
Through the maple trees,

And what will we see
In the trees, we three?

A small deer mouse,
And a hunting fox!

That's what we'll see
In the maple trees.

We'll all go exploring
Through the winter trees,

And what will we see
In the trees, we three?

A sleek, white weasel
And a timber wolf!

That's what we'll see
In the winter trees.

We'll all go exploring
In the land of trees,

My friend, Maggee,
And Jesse and me.

We'll All Go Exploring

Written by Maggee Spicer
and Richard Thompson

We'll all go exploring
In the world of trees,
My friend, Maggee,
And Jesse and me.

With their trunks and limbs,
With their roots and leaves…
Exploring together
Through the land of trees.

We'll all go exploring
Through the autumn trees,
And what will we see
In the trees, we three?

A quick-dart squirrel
And a chickadee!
That's what we'll see
In the autumn trees.

We'll all go exploring
In the dark spruce trees,
And what will we see
In the trees, we three?

A beaver, a moose,
And a Canada goose!
That's what we'll see
In the dark spruce trees.

We'll all go exploring
In the redwood trees,
And what will we see
In the trees, we three?

A marbled murrelet
And a spotted owl!
That's what we'll see
In the redwood trees.

We'll all go exploring
Through the old gum trees,
And what will we see
In the trees, we three?

A kookabura
And a koala bear!
That's what we'll see
In the old gum trees.

We'll all go exploring
Through the piñon trees,
And what will we see
In the trees, we three?

A swift road runner
And a rattlesnake!
That's what we'll see
In the piñon trees.

We'll all go exploring
Through the jungle trees,
And what will we see
In the trees, we three?

A spider monkey
And a lone jaguar!
That's what we'll see
In the jungle trees.

We'll all go exploring
Through the mangrove trees,
And what will we see
In the trees, we three?

A pink flamingo
And a crocodile!
That's what we'll see
In the mangrove trees.

We'll all go exploring
Through the apple trees,
And what will we see
In the trees, we three?

A raccoon bandit
And a hungry crow!
That's what we'll see
In the apple trees.

We'll all go exploring
Through the maple trees,
And what will we see
In the trees, we three?

A small deer mouse,
And a hunting fox!
That's what we'll see
In the maple trees.

We'll all go exploring
Through the winter trees,
And what will we see
In the trees, we three?

A sleek, white weasel
And a timber wolf!
That's what we'll see
In the winter trees.

We'll all go exploring
In the land of trees,
My friend, Maggee,
And Jesse and me.

We'll listen and watch
Then we'll come away,
So you can visit
On another day.